The Voice in the Jar

OrangeBooks Publication

1st Floor, Rajhans Arcade, Mall Road, Kohka, Bhilai, Chhattisgarh 490020

Website: **www.orangebooks.in**

First Edition, 2025

ISBN: 978-93-7426-497-3

Price: Rs. 220.00

Printed in India

The Voice In The Jar

Joe Nishmitha. V

OrangeBooks Publication
www.orangebooks.in

Contents

Chapter One

It all started when Meera heard the voice.

At fourteen years of age, Meera didn't consider herself quite so out of her wits that she would hear voices.

Although the people in the village thought otherwise…

Meera woke up in the morning as usual in her kudusai, the rustling of the leaves that made up her roof awaking her. She stretched her long limbs on the pai, tracing the intricate weave of the palm leaves with her fingers—the fibre tough and sturdy.

The sunlight was slowly creeping through the roof, gently stroking her face with warmth, like a loving mother. Well, she'd have to do with the sunlight's caress since she didn't have a mother.

Or a father.

But let's not dwell on that. She would rather not think about that.

You see, Meera was an orphan. But not the usual kind of orphan.

She wasn't born in the village like the other children were.

She was born in a basket.

At least, that was what her *appa* told her. Apparently, he had been going for another day of fishing when his hook caught something unexpected.

Her *appa* would beam, telling the story in his rough, sing-song voice:

> “And that’s when I saw you… wriggling and cooing in that basket. I had gone to get fish for another sell and bounty, but instead—” he would pull her into a cuddle, tickling her nose until she squealed—

> “—I found a priceless diamond instead.”

Five-year-old Meera would always giggle when he said it, tucked safe into his arms.

But the villagers didn’t think so.

Why?

Because of her eyes.

Bright golden eyes.

Far more golden than any other gold in the village.

She wasn’t a monster or a half-animal, not at all. She was quite lovely, her *appa* always assured her—a moon-like face, a starlit smile. Yet the villagers whispered. Whispered whenever her father took her into the village to sell fish.

People would look into her *appa’s* eyes, but never hers.

Meera remembered one incident particularly.

She had been sitting in the market with her *appa,* the myriads of goods being sold all around her, colourful woven mats being set up, the smell of fresh grain and jaggery wafting through the air. The stall next to her was owned by a mirror seller. He had brought his baby son that day, the infant wriggling on the mat, fists pumping, tiny face screwed in laughter.

Five-year-old Meera, wide-eyed and curious, had been instantly enamoured. She leaned forward, reaching out with all the innocent eagerness of a child.

Then—

**** SLAP. ****

The slap turned Meera's head sharply to the side. Her golden eyes widened, tears stinging unbidden. The mirror seller's wife hissed, clutching her infant close, her face screwed in fear and disgust.

- "Don't you dare touch him! With those eyes—those cursed—"

But she never finished.

Because Meera's *appa* intervened.

With the sweetest smile ever known to mankind, he rose from where he was gutting fish. He wiped his hands clean, then crouched to meet his daughter's trembling gaze.

- “Does it hurt, *kanna*?”

Meera shook her head, though her throat was tight.

Her father’s smile widened. He turned to the woman, his voice calm, almost musical as he began gutting another fresh batch of fish.

- “I would be careful, madam,” he said coolly, almost sweetly. “See, if you raise your hand like that…” His eyes twinkled. “It might just break and fall off.”

The entire market went silent.

His knife flashed.

- “I would know, you see. Gutting and everything… It’s all in the wrist.”

Nothing more happened.

The woman backed away, pale and stiff.

And Meera’s *appa* bundled her up on his shoulders and took her home, cheerfully humming as if nothing had occurred. That night, he gave her vellam, melting it into a syrup just for her. She fell asleep sweet and warm, her humiliation forgotten.

But she did remember, through her sleep, the sound of her *appa's* footsteps, heavy and purposeful, leaving the kudusai in the dead of night.

And the next morning, when she returned to the market with him, she noticed something strange.

No one avoided her eyes anymore.

The mirror seller's wife even gestured her over with an awkward smile.

- "Come here, *kanna.* How about a mirror for that pretty face, eh?"

Meera blinked, flabbergasted, still clutching her father's leg.

Her *appa* nudged her forward, beaming.

The woman held up her baby, rambling nervously, "Why don't you play with him, eh? He needs company."

The mirror seller nodded furiously, beaming in full agreement.

And then, one by one, other sellers nudged their children toward her.

Meera, bright-eyed and innocent, forgot everything and played happily, giggling with the other children, running around in circles.

And all the while, her *appa's* face softened with a strange, quiet pride.

All was well.

But sometimes, late at night, Meera wondered if her father's footsteps that night had meant something.

Years passed. The villagers treated her well.

Until her *appa* went missing.

He had gone fishing one night when she was twelve.

He never returned.

She had made her peace with it over the years. Perhaps he had drowned. Perhaps the waves had claimed him. She never, ever entertained the thought that he had abandoned her.

But sometimes, in the stillness of the kudusai, another thought crept in.

What if he had disappeared because of her?

What if the cursed child had finally taken the one person who had loved her?

And yet, she survived.

The villagers, to her surprise, were kind. Food and clothes appeared at her doorstep. Saris left folded, nets left mended. Perhaps it was for her. Perhaps it was in memory of her father.

But Meera noticed the sharpness in their eyes whenever she set up her stall.

The unspoken thought: *The cursed girl finally did it. Killed the one person who saw humanity in her.*

The very next morning, twelve-year-old Meera walked into the market calmly, set up her stall, and began gutting fish. Brutally, efficiently, just as her *appa* had taught her.

The entire market stared.

After that day, the sharp gleam in their eyes vanished.

Her stall had buyers again. Many, in fact.

“People love a cursed girl’s catch,” Meera often joked to herself.

Of course, she had friends too—her own age, younger, older. They never abandoned her.

And yet, despite all that, Meera always felt alone. Not just because she lived outside the village near the mangroves in her kudusai. Not just because she was different.

But because she had never truly belonged.

Still, she didn't bemoan her fate.

Her father had always said:

- "When you see the dark night, always look for the moon."

So, she did.

She started her day with her bath.

For Meera, a bath was a delight, a treat, not a chore—not at all. She followed the secret path only she knew (perks of having a kudusai out near the forest). She stepped carefully, mindful not to cut her feet on the jagged stones, and entered the mangrove path.

The trees stretched above her like the longest cave ever known. The air was still, smelling of damp and fresh soil. She waded into the pool, the coolness a gentle embrace.

Meera slipped in, humming softly. She pressed her palms together and offered a prayer to the mangrove spirits. She rinsed her hair, the cold water invigorating her skin.

And then, much to her surprise, a neelakurinji flower fell from the tree.

She inhaled. And for a moment, she was seven again.

Seven, cheeky and giggling in her father's arms, as he declared her the *alagu* (beauty) of the land while tucking the flower playfully in her hair.

The fragrance enveloped her nose, and so did the memory: sitting by the river with her *appa,* feet in the current, flicking water at each other until the air rang with laughter.

For a moment, with the neelakurinji flower in her hair, it felt like she was back there again.

Her eyes stung. She pressed the bloom to her nose and then— *"Meera …"*

The voice was soft and gentle, like a hush on a mangrove—barely heard, but there.

Meera froze, breath catching.

Nothing.

Then again: *Meera …*

This time it was thin, papery. Sharp, like a needle pricking.

A gust of cold air tugged her ear. Purposeful. Not the wind.

She jolted, almost falling into the river, clutching the root of a mangrove tree.

“Return to me …”

Her breath hitched. She dove her hand into her sack, fingers wrapping around the aruval (scythe). Her stance steadied, just as her *appa* had taught her long ago.

She waited.

No one.

Finally, she lowered the blade and returned to her kudusai.

She wished she could say that was the end of it.

It wasn’t.

Later, she went to her padagu tied carefully by the river. She unfurled the white sail, climbed aboard, and untied the rope. Ready with her vazhai, she pushed off.

The cool burst of air kissed her face as she adjusted the mundu of her podavai and cast the vazhai into the water.

Her *appa’s* memory struck her again—sternly ordering her to sit still while he cast the net, her knees hugged to her chest, her eyes wide as he grinned at a shoal of wriggling fish.

"The gods have blessed us well," he would say.

She ached for those days.

But then—the net grew heavier.

And heavier.

The reeds tightened, nearly snapping.

Meera gasped, pulling with all her strength. By the weight of it, this should have been a catch to feed half the village.

But it didn't rise.

It dragged her boat down.

And then—

"Meera …"

The sharp gust struck her ear again.

The reeds loosened. The weight vanished.

Trembling, she pulled the vazhai back and cast it again.

Trick of the mind. Trick of the mind …

But then she froze.

The water was clear.

And in it, the fish floated—staring at her. Their eyes fixed, unblinking.

And then, in a blink, the water was normal again.

Meera gasped, horrified.

When suddenly—

"Meera …"

This time, the whisper cut sharply, the wind needling her ear.

And suddenly, she wasn't so sure it was a trick of the mind anymore.

Chapter Two

Meera tried to steer her padagu back, breathing hard and shallow. She waved her hand over the river, as if she could brush away what she had seen.

“Nothing more than my mind… nothing more than my mind…” she muttered under her breath.

But something cold coiled in her chest.

And in her heart, she knew—this wasn’t normal.

She inhaled sharply, forcing a deep breath—

And then—

Splash.

The boat lurched violently. Meera flailed, gasping, but she immediately recovered her footing. She was a strong swimmer. Her *appa* had trained her in these very waters.

> "A fisherman must always have strong limbs, *kanna*," he had said once, voice booming, when he threw her into the river at eight years old. She had shrieked, flailing, certain she would drown. But she hadn't. She had clawed her way up, coughing, spluttering—breathing. Her *appa's* laughter had boomed across the banks, warm and loud.

> "See, Meera? You are a girl of a strong heart. A river girl."

> He had lifted her like a queen, his arms sturdy as he held her close, eyes softening.

> "The currents may be strong, but your hands will be your swords—if you will them to be."

Now, in the present, that memory thrummed through her veins.

Meera swam furiously.

But then she heard it again—

“Meera…”

Soft, cold, stabbing at her ear and crawling into her skull.

She gasped, kicking harder, eyes wide.

And then—she saw it.

The reflection in the water.

Her own face.

But it wasn’t her own.

Her golden eyes were glowing, dazed, otherworldly.

And the voice echoed sharper than before:

“Return to me…”

Suddenly, something coiled around her leg.

Meera screamed—but the sound was lost to the water as she was dragged down.

Her arms flailed, desperate, but the grip only tightened. Bubbles burst around her, slipping through her nose, her mouth, choking her.

From the corner of her eye, she saw shapes forming in the water.

Dark swirls.

Twisting around each other like snakes.

Murky, sinuous, coiling closer and closer.

Meera's eyes went wide. She tried to scream again, but only bubbles escaped.

She twisted, fought, thrashed—but nothing worked. She was stuck.

No… no, no! This can't happen. I can't die like this—I won't!

Her thoughts raced, wild, clawing for survival—

But the voice returned.

Sharp. Mocking.

- *"Oh, but you can. Perhaps this is your fate, girl of the river… to drown in the very waters your *appa* once spun you in."*

Meera froze, horror rattling her bones.

- *"Give up,"* the voice coaxed. *"No one would miss you. No one would mourn an orphan."*

Her body slackened.

The words, as grotesque as they were, wrapped around her like a lullaby.

- *"You could be with your *appa* again… you wouldn't be so lonely…"*

Her eyes fluttered closed.

Perhaps… perhaps it was right.

Perhaps—

Then another voice pierced through.

Her *appa's* voice.

Booming. Fierce.

- "You are a girl of the river, Meera! When the storm comes your way—you push past it!"

Her eyes snapped open.

Life thundered back into her veins.

She screamed underwater, twisting, kicking, clawing with every ounce of strength.

The grip on her leg loosened.

And then—

A golden burst of light exploded around her.

It shot from her very body, violent and dazzling, flooding the water with fire.

The shadows hissed, shuddered—then vanished, torn apart by the brilliance.

Meera kicked upwards, bursting through the surface. She gasped for air, chest heaving, eyes wild.

But then she froze.

The river was glowing.

A faint, golden shimmer illuminated the mangroves like scattered lanterns.

And when she caught her reflection—

Her own eyes glowed faintly back at her.

Golden.

Burning.

Chapter Three

Meera staggered back to the shore, coughing, her chest heaving, her lungs burning like fire. Her legs trembled as she dragged herself out of the water.

She froze.

Her paḍagu was sinking.

Meera's breath hitched. She screamed, desperate, flailing forward. She ran into the shallow waters, splashing, reaching out—

But she was too late.

Her padagu was gone.

Gone, as if it had never been.

The padagu… the same boat her *appa* had sailed since he was a boy.

- "It has been my friend, my saviour, my protector,"* he had always told her, gliding its sails with the tenderness of a man stroking a loved one. His eyes would twinkle as he added: *"People say it may be a piece of wood, but for me,

kanna… it is my friend."*

And she knew it was true.

The padagu had been her comfort, her last companion after her *appa* was gone.

It was the padagu she had sailed in countless times.

The padagu she had slept in on restless nights, gazing at the stars, whispering her thoughts to the wind.

And now… it was gone.

Meera's scream ripped through the mangroves.

Her knees buckled.

She collapsed, palms slapping against the softness of the mud. Her podavai clung to her body, soaked and heavy, but she used its edge to wipe her wet face. Her whole frame shook as she collapsed again, palms spread against the damp ground.

Her tears came hot, stinging, unstoppable.

It felt as if her heart had been torn clean from her chest.

Her breath came ragged, broken.

She closed her eyes.

But even in the darkness, she saw it.

That flash.

That golden light that had burst from her body, dazzling and wild.

How free it had made her feel.

If that thing—the shadow, the voice—came to her again, she vowed she would gut it alive. With the aruval, with her own bare hands, with whatever fire flowed through her veins.

Because in that moment… she had not felt fear.

She had felt free.

So free.

She inhaled sharply.

And then—

Once again—

“Meera…”

Meera stiffened.

But this time, she was no longer afraid.

Her hand shot to the aruval tucked in the folds of her podavai.

Her grip was tight.

Her stance is sure.

Her voice came out as a growl, sharp and furious:

“Who are you?! Who the hell are you?! *Paradesi!* *Naaye!* (dog!)”

Her screams echoed through the mangroves, carrying on the damp air.

Her chest heaved.

And then—

She saw it.

From the corner of her eye.

A flicker of motion.

A dark blur, darting between the trees.

Meera's eyes narrowed.

She raised the aruval higher.

Behind her, the river still shimmered faintly golden—remnants of the light still clinging to the water.

And before her—between the mangroves—something dark moved again.

Meera's ribs trembled with fear, but she breathed through it.

The aruval no longer felt like wood and steel. It felt like an extension of her arm.

She felt her *appa's* grip through it. His voice, fierce and comforting, rose in her memory:

- *"When the storm comes your way… You push past it."*

Her jaw clenched.

Her fear cracked like a tide breaking against rocks.

And Meera stepped forward.

Into the shadow.

Chapter Four

Meera expected a lot of things.

A beast crouched between the mangroves, waiting to devour her.

A spirit, thin and wraith-like, twisting through the leaves.

Or even a demon, come to drag her to the underworld.

But what she didn't expect to find was a jar.

It was half-buried within the roots of the mangrove.

Its brass head juts out.

But it was not brass.

It was glass.

The more she stared, the more wrong it felt.

The glass was clear.

Too clear.

Not like the fogged-up glass sold in the market, clouded with imperfections and tiny bubbles. This was sharp. Clean. *Too* clean. So, clear it looked as if the river itself had turned solid.

But that wasn't what caught her eye.

It was the carvings on the lid.

A lotus.

A yellow flower.

A jasmine.

Meera's breath hitched.

The symbols of the three fairy sisters.

Every child in the village had heard whispers of them. Even drunkards in the market mumbled their names.

Meera had first heard the story when she was five. She had fussed one night, sprawled on the mat in the kudusai, kicking her heels, chattering too much to sleep.

Her *appa* had sighed, pulled her close against his chest, and said playfully:

- "What if I tell you a story, *kanna*? Will you sleep then?"

She had stilled, wide-eyed in the darkness, and nodded.

And he told her this:

Long before the river cut the land, before the trees grew thick and tangled, there lived three fairy sisters.

Tamarai.

Malligai.

Roja.

Tamarai was the eldest: gentle, calm, and courageous. Her wings were as wide as a banyan leaf and more beautifully woven than the richest *pattu pavadai.* She was the keeper of healing, who could mend anything broken. Her people loved her. She was destined to be the fairy queen.

Malligai, the second, had wings as light and quick as a bird. She brought harvest, joy, and laughter wherever she went. She was loved for her good humour and her dancing heart.

And the youngest—Roja.

Small, slight, quiet. With a voice that could soothe and entice.

But unlike her sisters, Roja had no wings.

Yet she never let that trouble her, for her sisters' love was enough.

But the Witch Queen thought otherwise.

The Witch Queen, who dwelt between the rivers and the sea. If you looked upon her, you would see a woman beautiful and terrible: hair like raven tresses, eyes like sharp gold.

She had long despised the fairies.

And one twilight, she found Roja.

Sweet, lonely Roja—who wandered weeping to the edge of the river, mourning her bare back, while Tamarai's wings glowed like fire and Malligai's shone like pearl-drops.

The Witch Queen crouched beside her.

- "My child… why do you weep?"

And Roja should have turned away. But she didn't. She longed for someone—anyone—to whisper her pain to.

- "I have no wings… but my sisters do."

The Witch Queen comforted her, stroked her, soothed her.

And then she offered her a promise.

- "You can have wings too."

Roja froze, eyes wide.

The Witch Queen smiled, handed her a dagger, and whispered:

- "Dig out your sister's heart."

Roja shook her head, horrified.

- "I can't do that! They are my sisters!"

The Witch's voice was soft, persuasive.

- "But you will have them back. Eat the heart, and she will be reborn. And you will grow the most beautiful wings the world has ever seen."

Roja's heart screamed against it. She knew she shouldn't.

But her longing was too great.

What Roja forgot was this: Tamarai had wed. She had a husband, a fairy king. And she had borne a child, beloved though hidden from many.

But Roja didn't think of that. She only thought of wings.

So she cast a spell, and Tamarai fell into enchanted sleep.

Roja struck.

Malligai saw her sister's treachery. Horrified, she flew to warn the king.

But Roja turned on her too.

Malligai's scream tore through the palace. Her last words carried the truth to the king before she fell.

The fairy king froze, grief hollowing his soul. He hid his child. He hid the bloodline.

And Roja—Roja grew her wings.

Glorious, crimson-stained wings, as if painted with her sister's blood.

But the Witch had lied.

The wings came with madness.

Roja raged. She screamed, her voice cracking the skies, her mind broken.

Some say Malligai was killed. Some say she escaped. None knows.

But Roja?

They say she still flies.

They say she roams the skies in mad flight, her wings dripping red.

They say she still haunts these very forests.

They say the Witch Queen had a daughter, too.

They say Roja killed the Witch—but not her daughter.

And they say Roja still searches, hungry for blood, hungry for revenge.

Meera's breath hitched as the story came back to her, word for word, every detail her father once told her.

And then—the whisper again, sharp in her ear.

Her father had always said the Witch had eyes like sharp gold.

And he would always tease her, nuzzling her nose with a laugh:

- "Like yours, *kanna.* Sharp enough to cut."

Meera froze.

Her eyes.

Like hers.

Like hers.

Chapter Five

Meera had once heard that every person, in their life, carried a load of burdens on their shoulders.

That once they were done, they would heal.

They would feel relief.

They would find peace—apparently.

If Meera ever met the person who said that,

They were getting whacks with her aruval.

Peace?

Relief?

She looked down at her trembling hands,

Her knees sank into the damp mud.

Her padagu was gone.

Her *appa* was gone.

And now, apparently…

She was the daughter of a witch.

Ha.

The air felt warm around her.

The blue sky was slowly turning orange.

Time had passed—minutes or miles, she didn't know.

Meera didn't care.

Only one thought ran circles in her mind:

*Witch…

Witch…

Witch…

Witch.*

Meera inhaled— and then she screamed.

Birds burst from the mangroves, scattering into the sky.

"TAKE IT! TAKE IT ALL!

HAVEN'T YOU DONE IT ALL?!"

Her voice cracked, her breath hitched.

"I SAID TAKE IT ALL!

HAVEN'T YOU TAKEN IT ALL?!

HAVEN'T YOU?!"

Her voice crumbled. She inhaled sharply— And broke down.

Sobbing.

"Why…?

Why?

Please… take it.

Please…

Leave me alone…"

And then—

She felt it.

A faint hum.

Meera blinked.

She opened her tightly shut eyes.

And what she saw

Made her breath catch.

The jar—

Which had been empty before, Was now glowing.

Faint swirls of light turned within it,

Like fireflies trapped in glass.

Meera stared,

Breath - catching,

Unable to believe her own eyes.

Something inside her hardened.

She picked the jar up.

Her spine straightened.

And then— She heard it. *“Meera…”*

But this time, Meera did not flinch.

She did not grimace.

She did not hesitate.

She looked into the deep, dark forest and muttered,

“If I am the witch’s daughter…

She can come get me herself.”

Her grip tightened.

“But whatever this is…

I’m finding it out.”

And Meera set forward

On her path.

Chapter Six

Meera inhaled sharply, the taste of iron and blood in her mouth.

The jar was heavy in her hands, its brass head pressed against her teeth. Her jaw felt as though it were splintering, her skull pounding with an ache. Her fingers had gone numb, but still she tied her mundu tighter, adjusted her grip, and carried on.

She didn't dare loosen it.

Not when she felt the swirling inside.

At least the voices had stopped.

But the silence was far worse.

"*Meera…*"

There it was again.

Meera rolled her eyes skyward.

"Oh, here we go again," she muttered through clenched teeth.

"Always when I'm breaking my back."

Her jaw ached. Her arms screamed. Her legs squelched through the mud. But she stubbornly trudged on.

And then the questions came.

How had she never seen this before?

Was she truly the Witch's child?

The thought ate at her like a crow pecking at scraps.

The Witch had black hair. Meera had black hair.

But the Witch's skin was pale, white as a cloud.

Meera's was dusky, brown as wood.

Ah, whispered a voice in her mind, *witches can change their appearance. Perhaps you changed yours at birth. Perhaps you were once pale and white… but you disguised yourself to survive.*

She shook her head, gruffly, angrily, as if to fling the thought out of her skull.

When she was younger, Meera had liked to imagine she remembered her mother.

Vague, blurred images.

A kind smile.

A voice singing lullabies, soft and sweet.

Could a witch have done that? Truly?

Perhaps she could. Perhaps she had been both.

A mother.

And a monster.

A monster who sought to protect her blood while destroying others.

Meera drew in a shaky breath.

Did her *appa* know?

Had he always known?

Was that why he hid those warnings in stories, in songs, in laughter that was never just laughter?

Had he seen her as a monster, too?

The thought made her gasp in shame.

“No,” she whispered fiercely.

No.

Never.

Her *appa* had loved her. That was certain.

Perhaps he only wished to protect her.

She remembered his words:

- “Girl of the river. Eyes sharp enough to cut. Hold the aruval tight, *kanna.*”

The jar jolted in her hands.

The lid gave a furious twist.

The rose carved into the brass turned sharply, the whole jar shaking, trembling violently as though guiding her steps.

Meera froze, breath catching.

The jar was leading her.

Then—

Knock.

Her breath stilled.

She stared down at it.

Impossible.

Knock.

Again. Louder.

“Well, by the heavens,” she muttered, “if it does that again I’ll smash you over my own head.”

Knock.

Slow. Patient. Like someone knocking on a door.

She should throw it. Smash it. End it.

But instead, her thumb brushed the carvings—lotus, jasmine, rose.

And then a thought struck her like lightning.

Was it her?

Roja?

Chapter Seven

Meera stood for a moment, petrified.

The jar was warm and solid against her arms.

Her breath rattled and shattered in her throat. Her body seemed so frozen she could not even move.

Her *appa's* words echoed in her ear:

> "Keep in mind, my *kanna*... Roja is a fiery thing.

> A soft petal turned and purged due to grief.

> She is a fiery thorn.

> You either fight with all you have left—

> or you run."

Meera's eyes narrowed.

Well, she knew what she was doing.

Meera...

The whisper came in her ear—papery, soft.

Meera gritted her teeth.

Meera...

The voice again.

And again.

And again.

Like a sackcloth drawn tight around her skull.

Meera screamed.

“I am not scared of you! Do you hear me?!” Her eyes were wide, breathless, furious.

Her nails dug into the jar as she gasped for air and yelled again:

“Do you hear me?!

Do you hear me?!

You dog! You waste!”

Her voice rippled through the mangroves.

The wind rustled—as if in answer, as if supporting her.

And then—

A voice.

Sharper.

Closer.

Not mocking.

Urgent.

As if a warning.

“Look out…”

“Look out…” # Chapter Seven

Meera stood for a moment, petrified.

The jar was warm and solid against her arms.

Her breath rattled and shattered in her throat. Her body seemed so frozen that she could not even move.

Her *appa's* words echoed in her ear:

> "Keep in mind, my *kanna*… Roja is a fiery thing.

> A soft petal turned and purged due to grief.

> She is a fiery thorn.

> You either fight with all you have left—

> or you run."

Meera's eyes narrowed.

Well, she knew what she was doing.

Meera…

The whisper came in her ear—papery, soft.

Meera gritted her teeth.

Meera…

The voice again.

And again.

And again.

Like a sackcloth drawn tight around her skull.

Meera screamed.

“I am not scared of you! Do you hear me?!”

Her eyes were wide, breathless, furious.

Her nails dug into the jar as she gasped for air and yelled again:

“Do you hear me?!

Do you hear me?!

You dog! You waste!”

Her voice rippled through the mangroves.

The wind rustled—as if in answer, as if supporting her.

And then—

A voice.

Sharper.

Closer.

Not mocking.

Urgent.

As if a warning.

“Look out…”

“Look out…”

Chapter Eight

"Look out…"

Meera's eyes snapped open.

Her breath staggered violently in her throat.

She suddenly lost the ability to breathe.

She spun her head—searching and searching—

But nothing there…

Only the mangroves loomed around her,

Leaves whispering in the wind,

Nothing else.

But still, the voice continued to whisper in her ear, slowly—

“Look out… follow… don’t look back…”

Meera froze.

Her jaw clenched.

She took out her aruval.

The mangrove leaves gently fluttered in the wind

As if in warning.

And then the voice whispered again, soft—

“Look out… look out…”

The voice was layered now.

Doubled.

Meera’s eyes narrowed, clutching the jar.

“Fine…” she muttered.

"I am looking…"

But then—

Her skin prickled.

The air turned dangerously cold.

Meera froze.

Okay…

This was new.

The leaves rustled slowly,

But it was as if the air itself darkened.

The vines on the trees

Began to sway

In the most haunting rhythm.

Meera stood, eyes wide.

And then—whispers.

Not just one.

But multiple.

In her head.

Meera gasped, almost dropping the jar.

It stung through her skull like—

A sword.

Incoherent whispers.

Insistent.

Furious.

"Meera…

Meera…

Meera…

Meera…"

And then—

The vines slowly began to rise.

Twisting.

Coiling around each other.

Meera froze, eyes wide, stunned.

She did not realise what it was forming.

The jar in her hands shook violently.

Quivering in fear.

Her fingers spasmed.

She nearly dropped it.

Then—

Meera…

Meera…

MEERA!

They were no longer whispers.

There were screams.

In her head.

She gasped, falling to the ground,

Clutching her skull.

“STOP IT!

STOP IT!”

The vines coiled like snakes,

Twisting, bending, more and more—

And then forming—

A figure.

A horrible bloom of vines.

A stem rising…

Two shoulders.

A torso.

A head.

Meera froze.

She was on the ground, unable to move.

But still— She grabbed her aruval,

Pointing it furiously at the figure.

“STAY BACK!” she yelled.

“STAY BACK!”

The figure leaned toward her.

Meera slashed, wild and fierce—

“STAY BACK, I SAY!!!”

And then—

The other whispers from the jar

Rose like a storm:

“RUN!

RUN!”

And then—

The chest of the figure

Began to split…

And in the blink of an eye—

It was gone.

Meera stared, eyes wide.

The forest was bright again.

No cold wind.

She drew a shaky breath, pushing herself up.

She hesitantly picked up the jar.

It was normal again.

The swirling was peaceful—almost calm.

Meera expected the energy to still.

But it didn't.

It slowed.

But it did not leave.

The energy thrummed.

Once.

Twice.

The swirling grew faster.

Meera's breath hitched.

And then the voice whispered again.

Softer.

Gentle.

Like the breeze across the mangroves.

"Look out…

Don't look back…

Move on…

Please…"

Soft.

Fragile.

Terrified.

"Who are you?" she whispered.

Silence.

No reply.

Meera's eye twitched.

Seriously?!

But at this point, she only sighed

And walked on.

She jostled the jar in irritation.

“When I find whoever you are,

We are going to have a lot to talk about.”

The End

Chapter Nine

Meera slashed through the roots.

The aruval cut deep, hacking through the tendrils.

The tendrils snapped.

She felt a strange sense of vindication when she did.

Perhaps they were shaped like snarled hands,

Waiting to stop her.

She had tied the aruval into her mundu carefully.

The forest's path seemed strangely freer now.

Roots no longer strangled her feet.

She blinked in confusion at first

When she saw the glow.

The glow of the jar

Within her mundu.

She froze.

Oh…

She clenched the aruval between her teeth,

Using her pallu to fasten the jar tightly,

Making sure it wouldn't fall.

It throbbed. Not violently now—

But steadily.

Like a heartbeat.

Meera huffed and walked on.

She hummed a song to keep her spirit up:

> *"Oh, Chandra, won't you show your face*

> *Hiding behind the window of your moonlight pane*

> *How long will we wait a while?*

> *To see your eyes and lovely smile…"*

She hummed,

Trying hard to take her mind off things.

But the jar

It was still thrumming.

As if humming along to her.

Meera raised an eyebrow.

"Oh, don't get too smug with me."

The jar pulsed—

A single beat.

As if taunting her.

Meera rolled her eyes playfully. Her lips tugged into a rare smile.

As she trudged on.

The mud softened beneath her steps.

The path widened—

Just a little.

Subtle.

But real.

She froze, drawing a breath.

Alright.

Alright.

She was not panicking.

Definitely not panicking at all…

The jar gave a little shake.

Meera lifted her eyebrow again.

"Oh, don't play coy with me…"

Another hum.

Meera added pleasantly,

"If I ever find who you are,

Glass kutty,

I'm throwing you in the river…" She added this with mock cheerfulness.

The jar hummed— As if taunting her back.

Meera's lips curled into a sly grin.

“Ah, so you *did* hear me?”

And then—

Run…

Don’t look back…

Meera froze.

But only for a moment.

She drew a slow breath.

“I won’t.”

And she walked on.

The End

Chapter Ten

Meera walked on.

She knew this place.

She had gone past these paths many times— To collect berries, to gather mangoes.

The tree with branches like snarled hands.

The stump is shaped like a horse.

Years…

The jar turned.

Defiant.

Guiding her.

Guiding her **past the boundary of the village.** Meera froze as she realised—

This part of the forest did not belong to men.

Or anyone.

She inhaled sharply, gripping the glass jar.

"Oh, you really have a bloody sense of humour, don't you, glass kutty?

One kick I will nicely give you, uh?"

The glass shimmered furiously,

The swirling dancing like a jackal.

Meera looked up.

Swallowed.

"Fine…" she muttered.

Despite every instinct screaming at her to run—

She walked deeper.

Deeper.

The mangroves began to disappear,

Little by little…

And new trees

Unfolded before her.

She stepped forward.

No ground.

No mud.

Only dry moss.

The trees here were different.

Taller.

Leafless.

Bark like stone,

Stretching to the sky—

Forming around her

Like the ribs of a cave.

Meera inhaled deeply.

But then she noticed—

Her breath had turned cold.

She glanced down.

The jar was glowing against her mundu,

Thrumming like a heartbeat against her ribs.

The lid was turning.

She could feel it.

She froze.

Breath - catching.

She must be getting nearer.

She muttered, low and irritated,

“A bloody sense of humour you have…

If anything comes, I’m throwing you straight in its mouth first…”

She walked.

On.

Each step—

Soundless.

She froze.

She hadn’t realised until now…

There was **no thump** of her feet.

No crack of twig.

No rustle.

Just air.

Merely air…

Silence pressed against her

From all sides,

Like a tangled mat of night.

It was calm.

Too calm.

Her footsteps left no marks.

As if she were walking on air.

And then…

She began to wonder.

Why had the glow—

That golden blaze in the river— Never returned to her hands?

Why?

When she had been drowning,

Struggling for life…

It burst out of her.

Free.

So why now—

Nothing?

Well, she thought grimly, if something came for her again,

Even the aruval might not be enough.

She hesitated.

Then—

She sat down on the road.

(Yes. On the road. Don't laugh.)

She began to twirl her hands, slowly,

In a weaving motion.

Nothing happened.

For a long while.

Frustration tightened in her chest,

Coiling like a fist—

And then—

A voice.

In her head.

Calm.

Smooth.

- “Twist your hands…”

Meera froze.

The glow in the jar twisted in a circular motion.

She followed it with her fingers.

And then—

Nothing.

Meera’s fury flared.

She was ready to hurl the jar at a tree—

When suddenly—

A spark.

So small

It could have been missed.

Then another.

Then a few.

Then—

A first coil of light.

The End

Chapter Eleven

Meera stared.

Wide-eyed.

In delight.

A laugh — small and breathless —

Slipped from her lips

Before she could stop it.

There it was.

Not a trick of water.

Not out of panic.

Pure light.

Real light.

Curling and coiling through her hands like a rope.

“Well, I’ll be damned…”

The jar thrummed,

Its pulse is slow and steady —

Wriggling,

As if to say,

“Well done.”

She laughed softly.

“You know…” she muttered,

“I can’t believe I’m saying this,

But I think I’m growing fond of you…”

The glass stilled…Then thrummed again,

As if touched.

Meera grinned,

Warmth blooming in her chest.

And then—

The light grew brighter.

And brighter.

Chapter Twelve

The light grew brighter.

And brighter.

Meera squinted —

Not even the least bit panicked.

That was her first mistake.

That must have been her first warning.

The light crawled across her skin,

Soft as a breath at first.

Then — Pulsing.

Crack.

Somewhere in the forest.

Meera froze, eyes wide,

Noticing a split forming across the smooth ground.

Her hand flew to her aruval.

The light did not disappear.

Instead…

It grew brighter.

Even as shadows crept across the earth,

The light spread —

Like vines.

Stark against the pale ground,

Creeping slowly, steadily.

Meera flipped her aruval into position.

And then she looked up.

What she saw

Made her freeze.

In front of her stood a woman.

Sweet.

Desolate.

Tall and lithe.

With soft eyes,

Skin dusky as bronze.

She wore a pale pink dress,

Torn at the edges —

Like flower petals.

A whiff of lotus

Drifted through the air.

Meera’s breath hitched. **Tamarai.**

She stiffened.

What should she do?

Fight?

But Tamarai…

Had other plans.

The woman's lips trembled

Into a shaky smile.

She lifted one hand —

Gentle, trembling.

And whispered,

"You have returned…"

And in the blink of an eye —

She disappeared.

Chapter Thirteen

Meera blinked.

Well… that was not strange, apparently.

But apparently, today it had no plans of leaving her alone.

She got to her feet, tucked the jar into her sari,

Tied her mundu firmly.

She reached to tuck her aruval back in—

She didn't need to.

Because standing

In front of her

Was

A spectre so horrifying

Her stomach turned.

It did not move.

It did not speak.

It was a black mass.

Black nerves.

She couldn't tell.

It wriggled

And wriggled—

And shaped itself into a…

Woman.

Hair flying everywhere.

No eyes.

No nose.

No mouth.

But then—

A slit.

White.

Pure white.

Opening on its face

Like a grotesque smile.

Stark.

Against the darkness of its skin.

Meera did not breathe.

She did not blink.

She was too stunned to do so.

The name died.

Before it could form on her tongue.

She knew one thing:

If she named it—

She was dead.

Some things.

Weren’t meant to be named.

Not if she wished to leave.

She drew a breath,

Slowly backing away.

The thing followed her.

The slit on its face

Growing wider…

And wider…

Meera had a plan.

She was going to summon the light,

Strike it with her aruval—

When—

It screamed.

That unholy scream.

Meera would never forget it.

She gasped,

Her skull splitting from the impact, her eyes burning,

Her nose aflame.

Her knees buckled.

The creature screamed.

And Meera's mind

Ran with a plan.

She crumpled to the ground,

Snapped her eyes shut…

And waited.

And waited.

She felt it.

The creature.

Slowly

Coming towards her.

She felt it.

Leaning down.

She drew a breath—

AND SHOT UP

With a yell.

Aruval in hand.

No fear.

She did not let it in.

Only a **ferocious desire.** She willed it—

The light.

Through her body.

To her arms.

To her blade.

****SLASH.****

She struck it.

Straight through the heart.

She knew:

No matter how powerful a creature—

The heart was always its weakness.

She used it.

Nothing happened.

For a moment.

Then—

An unholy scream.

The creature

Crumpled to dust.

Chapter Fourteen

The dust of the creature had barely faded

When Meera felt it—

A heavy, lurching sense of giddiness,

As if the power inside her

Had reached out

And taken its due.

The jar thrummed faintly.

Not in her hands.

In her.

She fell to her knees.

Her leg hit the ground softly.

And a voice— Inside her head— Whispered gently:

Rest now.

Meera had never known sleep like that.

Not once in her life.

It was dark.

And dreamless.

She had *never* dreamt without fear.

But this— This was nothing.

No river.

No forest.

No jar.

Only dark.

And then—

The darkness shifted.

Pure light.

And then she was there…

Meera's breath caught.

There, in the distance,

Stood a **white figure**.

Still.

Silent.

"Who…?" she whispered.

The figure did not move.

But a voice—not from it,   But **inside her skull**—

Whispered:

"Don't let *her* find you."

Meera blinked.

"Well… that was comforting," she muttered dryly.

The voice—   Sudden. Sharp.

"DON'T LET HER NAME YOU!"

Meera froze, eyes wide.

And then another bright light—

She was lifted into the air

At lightning speed.

Meera's body went still— She wasn't able to move or speak.

She was thrown up in the air like a rag doll.

She opened her mouth to scream,

To gasp,

To make a sound—

But she couldn't.

And then the white disappeared.

And then—

She found herself in a room.

A black, dark room.

Until it cleared.

And her breath—

Hitched.

It was the most beautiful room she had ever seen.

Marble walls and pillars,

Designs carved in each one of them… Not just designs—

stories.

Scenes

From the tales

She had only heard…

Wild monsters being vanquished by heroes,

Heroes are going on the journey,

And fairies bless them.

Fairies.

Meera suddenly had a good idea

Where she was…

And then she heard—

A breathing.

Shallow breathing.

Meera blinked

And turned toward the sound—

And immediately,

The soul went out of her body.

A girl stood in front of her.

No—

A creature, more like it!

Hair thrown over her head,

Only horrible red eyes

With dots for pupils.

Wings—

Beautiful wings— But misshapen, horrible.

White, pale arms creeping out of her gown

Made of withered roses.

Meera froze, eyes wide.

"Ro—"

But the name died in her mind.

The figure didn't seem to hear her.

She took a hand— A bloodied, pale hand—

And rubbed it on the marble halls,

Staining the carved legends

With blood.

"Blood is nothing more than poison," she murmured. "Friendship—a noose on your neck."

Meera blinked.

Yes—

The girl seemed like she loved her family, alright.

But then she looked up at Meera.

Meera froze, body going stiff as a log.

What?!

She thought this was a *scene*—

Not—

But then—

She tilted her head.

“All is not what it seems.

Not what you think.”

Meera jolted back into her body

Like a fish dragged from water— Eyes wide, gasping.

She was awake.

Alive.

A *renewed* energy

Blazing in her veins.

The jar glowed bright.

Meera blinked, dazed, realising—

The ache in her bones was gone.

The bleeding had stopped.

The jar continued to thrum—

Furiously.

Meera murmured, soft and soothing:

“It’s alright…

You can breathe now.”

But the jar did **not** calm.

Meera understood why—

Because the forest

Was slowly

Darkening.

With **thorns.**

Black.

Coiling and twisting around each other

In the most horrifying manner

That made Meera queasy.

Meera stared.

"Well," she muttered flatly,

"This is just brilliant."

Chapter Fifteen

Meera gasped, eyes wide.

The thorns were everywhere.

She slashed with her aruval,

Furiously hacking— But they moved faster,

Twisting like snakes.

One clamped around her leg.

Another around her arms.

Before she could blink—

She was bound.

They coiled up her body,

Tight… tighter…

Brutally digging in.

Her ribs screamed. Her neck was yanked back, forced to face the sky.

Like they wanted her to kneel.

Like they wanted her to beg.

For the first time in her life—

It looked like she did not have

A way out.

A voice slithered through her skull:

- "Brave, brave child of the gold…

You are just like your mother."

Meera’s blood boiled.

Her mind roared:

> *I am not my mother.*

> *I am not my mother.*

> *I will NEVER be my mother.*

But all she tasted—

Was blood.

The voice curled closer:

➢ “River girl…

Let’s see how long you last

Before you break…”

Meera’s vision

Cracked into black.

She heard them then.

The villagers— Their whispers, their shame.

➢ “Cursed.”

“Disgusting.”

“Freak.”

“Her father should’ve left her in the river.”

"She wasn't meant to live…"

She could not move.

Could not breathe.

And then—

Something snapped

Inside her.

Not fear.

Rage.

Meera did not scream in fear.

She screamed

Like war.

The thorns pulled tighter—

Slicing into her flesh.

"Pull harder," she thought savagely. "Make me bleed."

"I am the daughter of the river—

Unbowed, unbent, unbroken."

Her muscles locked— then exploded.

The vines,

****SNAPPED****

Like brittle sticks.

"You think you can break me?!"

She roared.

"DO YOU?!"

She spun her aruval—

Not like a blade—

Like a **promise.**

And then she charged.

Feet pounding.

Not a girl.

Not a fisher child.

A storm.

A fire.

A whirlpool unleashed.

Every strike split the air

Like thunder through bone.

She wasn't fighting to live.

She was fighting to **end** this.

She might have been.

The Witch's daughter—

But she refused.

To be another dark tale.

She was going to break it.

Rewrite it.

She screamed.

Her vision blazed back— Light tearing through her veins,

Wild, uncontrollable.

The thorns shattered.

They regrew.

Stronger.

Angrier.

But something had changed

In Meera.

She fought.

Like she was born for it.

Not against the forest—

against fate.

- "YOU WANT TO BREAK ME?!" she roared.

"COME ON!"

"I'M NOT SCARED OF YOU!"

"NOT ANYMORE!"

"NOT ANY LONGER!"

The thorns recoiled—

Retreating, writhing,

Forming a massive wall…

A mountain of darkness

Rising to swallow her whole.

But Meera—

She *leapt.*

High.

Aruval raised.

Blood in her mouth.

Fire in her bones.

And she **slashed**

Through it all.

That was the last thing she saw.

Because her vision

Went pure white.

And the last thing she heard—

A soft, sweet voice:

- You did well, little one.

Chapter Sixteen

Meera's eyes remained in the dark for a while.

Everything was black.

Her body regained its alertness,

But her vision stayed blurred.

Was she still asleep?

Soon, it cleared.

She blinked.

She was lying on a warm, soft mattress—

No.

Not a mattress.

It felt like she rested upon a cloud.

Her wounds were bandaged.

She no longer felt like she was being skinned alive.

Hell… she only felt a heavy tiredness.

She froze when she no longer felt the weight

Of the jar at her mundu.

She tried to lift her body—

But she couldn't.

She glanced around desperately.

She should be scared.

She should be terrified.

But no.

Instead—

She felt a damned, wretched peacefulness.

And then she saw it.

The jar.

Beside her.

But it did not fill her with joy.

It filled her with horror.

Why?

The jar was completely broken.

Cracked.

No longer any magic swirling inside it.

Meera gasped.

No…

No…

No.

But then—

She heard a gentle voice.

“Don’t worry…

You have succeeded in your mission.”

Meera blinked.

There she was.

A woman.

Tall.

Black-haired.

Worn at the edges, yet quietly lovely,

Her face pale as snow.

Her hair flowed down to her legs,

And her eyes were green,

Like fresh mangrove leaves.

She wore a long pavadai

Of blue and gold.

But… there was something about her.

Shimmers floated around her—

The same shimmers

That had spilt

From Meera's own hands.

The woman smiled brightly.

"Ah! You are awake. Splendid!"

Meera blinked.

"W-who are you?"

The lady raised a playful eyebrow— And instantly, a scent brushed Meera's nose.

Jasmine.

"Malligai…" Meera whispered.

The woman's smile turned wry, yet pleased.

"It feels like music…

Hearing that name again after so long."

But Malligai blinked in surprise

When Meera dropped to her knees.

Meera trembled.

"I'm sorry… I'm sorry.

I saw what my mother did to you…"

Malligai stared, flabbergasted.

"Yemmadi, what is this?"

"But… but I'm the witch's daughter—

The one who broke your family."

Malligai looked at her for a long moment, then sighed.

"And where did you get *that* idea?"

She muttered, rubbing her forehead.

Meera blinked.

"My eyes… they're gold, like—"

Malligai inhaled softly.

"Ah. Tales spread truth…

But twist it too.

Gold eyes did not belong to the witch.

They belonged to the Queen of the Faeries.

My sister.

My akka."

It did not strike Meera at first—

And then it froze her blood.

Malligai leaned forward,

Cupping Meera's face,

Her fingers were trembling.

"I have not seen you," she whispered,

"Not since you went out,

With your father that night…"

Meera's breath hitched, shallow.

She shut her eyes, gasping—

Tears spilling fast.

Malligai pulled her in gently.

"Sweet thing…"

Her voice shook.

"Oh, poor thing. I'm so sorry."

Meera stiffened—

Then clung to Malligai with all her strength,

Sobbing.

Embarrassingly.

Desperately.

Like a child starved of touch.

When they finally pulled apart, Meera murmured,

"I don't understand…

They said you died that night…"

Malligai's expression darkened.

"I…"

She let out a soft, bitter laugh.

"After my sister struck me down— After I warned your father—

I fled to the human lands.

I knew my sister's mind was lost.

If I were found…

My wings, my blood…

Could be used for more destruction."

She inhaled.

"So, I cut them off myself."

Meera froze.

"You… you cut them?"

Malligai chuckled softly.

"Don't worry, *kanna.*

I kept most of my magic.

But… my sister found me again.

I was of no use to her now.

So, she bound me to this cottage.

She thought you died.

I did not seek to correct her."

Malligai inhaled deeply.

"And I did not know where you were, either.

But I couldn't…"

Her expression darkened.

"My sister bound me here.

Unless my own blood came…

I could not leave."

Meera froze, breath catching.

She opened her mouth—

But Malligai continued.

"Ah… how did I find you?

And the jar?" She smiled faintly.

"I didn't. Not truly.

But then… I sensed you."

Meera blinked.

"Sensed me?"

Malligai nodded. "A faerie can always sense,

Another faerie's essence.

Their life-force.

Their magic.

I thought it was imagination at first…" She smiled tearfully.

"But it wasn't.

As you grew,

I realised you were alive.

And I finally gained the strength to fight.

To reach you."

Meera froze. "The jar… it was you." She winced.

"So, uh… You heard?"

Malligai raised an eyebrow.

"About how you threatened to kick me?"

"Yes."

Meera groaned.

Malligai laughed.

But then—

Malligai looked into Meera's eyes.

"But now Roja knows you live.

That Tamarai's blood lives.

And she will come for you.

The war will come."

Meera's ribcage tightened.

"A war?"

Malligai's eyes glimmered.

"The dark age is over,"

She murmured cryptically.

“The light must be won.”

Meera hesitated.

“And… the witch?

She was the one who—”

Malligai looked at her gently.

“My sweet girl. Every tale has someone who is called rotten.

But sometimes…

They are not villains at all.” Meera stared, bewildered.

“Right,” she whispered weakly.

“So… I must fight my own aunt?”

Malligai laughed softly.

“Cheeky thing.

You will rest first.

Battles will be taught later.”

Meera opened her mouth to protest—

But Malligai tapped her forehead.

Her eyes fluttered.

Sleep pulled her under.

Meera knew her life.

It would never be the same.

But for the first time—

Light,

And flight,

Bloomed inside her.

The End